Along comes a girl called Goldilocks,
wearing her favourite red-and-blue socks.
She walks right in — the girl never knocks!
Her manners are gone — she forgot 'em!

She looks for some porridge, and guess what
One is too cold and one is too hot.
The last is just right, so she gobbles the lot.
What a bad little girl — she's rotten!

Feeling full up, she wants to sit down.
"Too hard! Too soft!" she says with a frown.
She tries Baby's chair and ends upside down!
Crash! She's gone through the bottom!

Sleepy, Goldilocks goes up to bed.
Too high, too low, both beds hurt her head.
So she picks the little bear's bed instead.
(She likes the sheets — they are cotton.)

Zzzz!

Zzzzzz!

The bears come home. The bears are mad!
"Someone's been eating my porridge," says Dad.
"Mine too," says Mum. "And mine," says their lad.
"She's eaten it right to the bottom!"

"Someone's been sitting in my chair, too,"
says Dad, then Mum, "Oh, what shall we do?"
"And my chair's broken. Boohoo! It was new!"
cries sad little Baby Bear Bottom.

They race up the stairs, and hearing a knock,
Goldilocks suddenly wakes with a shock!
Baby Bear screams, and she's up like a shot,
"There's the intruder — we've got 'em!"

She jumps from the window and runs away!
She's learning a lot about bears today —
their beds, their chairs and to stay far away
from the porridge of Baby Bear Bottom!

Eek!